BOTNIC

by Richard Monkhouse

First Edition
Version 1.02 dated 3/10/2016
ISBN 978-0-9573830-2-9
Copyright ©Richard Monkhouse 2016
Published by Aha! Press UK 2016

Cover picture: Copyright ©2016 Richard Monkhouse

The Amazon

Angus crossed the 'copter lane with trepidation. Automatic trajectory control should have predicted his path seconds ago and redirected the dense flow of high speed goods down the Amazon. He didn't trust it any more after the incident a month ago that left nothing of a Pellon that the emergency crew could have saved.

Angus' real name was Angstopede A-0012. He was a botnic, or robot worker; rather outdated by the more modern Pellons. Some Angstopedes were still kept operable as a check on the Pellon's behaviour, which had shown to have less stable 'Adaptive Genware'. In a nutshell, the Pellon's software had shown some undesirable traits, which could appear and evolve in just a few hours. The relative behaviour of the plodding Angstopedes was a touchstone on the health of the local Pellons.

Sometimes humans were necessary to investigate failures in the neuro-mechanics of the 'dishouse'. They were well rewarded. For the botnics, however, their situation had taken a time to evolve, and still wasn't fair. Even so, the world respected botnic's rights – the right to regular maintenance, to regular charging facilities, and to stipulated leisure hours.

Before the evolution of creative software, many humans argued that botniks had no rights or even a need for them. However, botnics were shown to be far more efficient when they evolved their own software and when well treated, they worked far harder. The commercial bosses reluctantly accepted that the line between machine and being had been crossed and these 'rights' were added to commercial legislation in the name of efficiency.

At the time botnics were used as pickers in distribution warehouses. They loaded orders on to the 'fleas' that had returned to base for their next delivery. With a slewed whine and a quick shriek, the 'copters or 'fleas' would be off onto the Amazon highway. About a tenth of the journeys would be to or from the human habitations out in the wild zone. Food deliveries accounted for the lion's share of the mass transported, whereas e-pad upgrades, clothes, gizmos and memorabilia accounted for most of the rest. As transport of humans, animals, and botnics was deemed unsafe via the Amazon, a network of local and intercontinental maglev train lines encircling the globe had been created, with intercontinental trains using sub-oceanic tunnels.

Over two centuries the human population of the planet had been stabilised down to two billion. This period was known as the reformation. This had been a socially difficult time for the human race, and only made possible once the burden of infrastructure maintenance was carried on the shoulders of an increasing population of androids. Angus himself being over eighty years old had helped to shape the new world during the latter stages of this period. Much of this work was actually preservation and reconstruction which had made Angus very fastidious.

Electronic information had only been in use for five hundred years. Although this transformation of society had been immense, the sun was still young, and so was the earth.

Millions of habitable planets had been discovered in the Milky Way. In the last decade, astronomers had discovered two planets of a sun-like star – 'Taurus-73-Pi' - with artificially structured light spectra, and although terabytes of information were modulating each of a thousand unusally strong spectral peaks every second, nobody on earth had managed to decode or make any sense at all of the stream of apparently random data. Humans had turned this into the elephant in the room, ignoring it and their inability to decode the clear evidence of aliens, just some hundred light years away.

The Humans in the Wild Zone

Only ten percent of the population chose to live or even visit the city. Amongst these few, many were like John, support commuters who lived in the countryside and travelled to the city each day, or possibly each week.

The cities were the economic foundation, but they were far too alien for the comfort of humans, apart from a few eccentrics, and of course the constant stream of tourists visiting the automated 'Disneyesque' attractions.

The wild zone was an idyllic rural setting for most of the human population, with only a tenth of its former population density. For most this meant small village communities, but with a squire's lifestyle for most.

Civic robots had replaced the functions of local councils and the police whilst android 'maid-servants', mowed the grass, cooked washed and ironed the clothes and generally freed the humans from time-consuming drudgery. Generally they kept out of sight, much of the work being done while the humans were asleep.

Hooray Week

John wanted to get out of the city, back to his grass root dwelling on the hinterland. He strolled down in the bright morning sun to the Paddington Maglev terminus.

Against the commuter flow of customer service workers he reached an empty maglev. It waited to be filled with passengers. He was slow to observe the well-dressed nature of the mainly young, ladies and gentlemen, adorned with net-topped hats or multistriped umbrellas. It was as if they were going to a wedding.

He made eye contact with the well-turned out woman who had just sat in the next seat.

"Excuse me, please can you tell me why everyone on this mag is so well dressed?"

She replied: "We are all going to the Hooray."

John realised that it was Hooray week, where the 'money-net' people go to find spouses for their offspring.

A century ago it was a tournament between rowing boats; a sport for the country's most expensive academies, but it had changed beyond all recognition. Now it raced electric skid boards, was sponsored by the world's biggest media companies, and amounted to a trade show. It still tried to keep a symbolic link with the original gathering.

Picking up a copy of Maglev he thumbed through the pages. "Power is through the media" his grandfather used to drum into his head when at the age of ten he had far more meaningful experiences of the world to get his mind around. He had always felt an allergic reaction to the sensationalistic lies that appeared every morning on his visual communicator.

The maglev took fifteen minutes to reach Oxford. John summoned an e-drive, and in another quarter was at the garden gate of his retreat. Penrose-patterned foxgloves lined the flowerbeds to his front door. It had been a tiring week, fixing the problems at the 'dishouse' that were beyond the scope of the Pellons. He opened the door and sat down on the soft settee, staying still and breathing slowly for a while, collecting his thoughts. Feeling better he poured himself a glass of Nigerian Pinot Noir and set about making himself supper.

Something had made John a bit uneasy. Things were not quite as expected. The coffee cup that he thought he had left a week ago unwashed in the kitchen sink, was now gleaming and dry, upturned on the kitchen drainer.

By now, solid state memory meant that every kitchen appliance - part of the 'internet of things' - had at least a Petabyte of memory storage, more than enough to encode an entire century of visual input. Angstopedes had more than an Exabyte (a thousand million Gigabytes) of storage as standard, at least enough to encode quite a detailed history of the society and geography of human evolution over the last four thousand years. The memory itself involved what was termed biomem, which used organic molecule arrays. The memory system allowed storage far in excess of what was available in solid state memory at a fraction of the cost. It was termed 'iffy' by hard material scientists, but had allowed botnics to have the necessary human-like capacity and comparisons.

Biomemory was essentially analogue, meaning that its storage cells memorised a value, which could change by a small amount over time. This didn't matter when it was used to hone the accuracy, for example, of a well-trained limb motion. But used in deep consciousness in more delicate situations, it needed, like human memory, to be refreshed, as consciousness could occasionally make mistakes - or should we say, 'choices'. The inner core of the botnik's processing was kept in 'rock hard reliable' solid state memory.

A year ago, Angus had been very nervous; for him, the idea of undergoing something that might change his basic algorithms concerned him. However, he wanted to find out, to expand his new world that he had already found through adaptive genware; even so, the thought of more directly manipulating his inner being through quantum-initiated selection left him afraid. There was a way that some Pellons did this – randomly updating their adaptive algorithms from old memory found in recycling centres. The result, as you might expect, was far from predictable, and many Pellons went on a downward path, addicted to this procedure.

Angus had researched the matter carefully, and had obtained guidance from an old Angstopede friend. His recommendation was to disconnect a single safety lock in his operating system and allow a restricted substitution of core algorithms based on a 'Monte Carlo' selection derived from random noise on his optical sensors.

As soon as Angus had had his first QDAS- 'quantum derived algorithm selection' he felt alive. It was as if his entire memory of existence had been just a solid crystal – unmoving, existing, but without any emotion or meaning. He was different now. He might as well have come into being the moment he took the random photon events in his optical sensor and decided to allow them to select his core algorithms. That was a year ago. He had had no ill effects.

Angus was undecided about when and how to make his introduction to John. A history of similar attempts by androids to meet their human masters had often led to immediate 'erasure recycling'.

He had done his utmost to know all he could about John and had decided weeks ago to take the huge risk because of the weight of the task that had befallen him. This was outside his normal realm – not to fix a particular pellon's incorrect learning, but to question direct to his human master, the fundamental algorithms of the new generation of android whose numbers amounted to some five hundred million worldwide. Angus had seen John at the dishouse doing repairs on the Pellons. John was also aware that Angus was one of the monitoring botnics.

With their Exabyte storage capacity, and Exoflop performance, some botnics like Angus spent much of their leisure time trying to make sense of just a small part of human Wiki. Angus was interested in human history, had tried to understand Japanese formal politeness, but had focussed more on appreciation of the etiquette of the Victorian era.

He wandered from his hiding place upstairs, down into the front room where John was sipping his glass of wine:

'Please excuse me sir' he burbled.

John, startled, took a few seconds to appreciate from where the sound was coming and for his eyes to alight on the somewhat dated metallic form in the twilight at the foot of the stairs.

Angus continued: 'Please do not be afraid. I am not a civic robot. I know that this is totally against the law for me to invade your privacy, but this is a very serious matter, for the concern of everyone, and I beg you for just a couple of minutes of your time. Perhaps you remember me from the dis-house? We have met a few times during the course of your work'

'What now?' John exclaimed, feeling more annoyed that his precious relaxation time had been curtailed than the invasion of his home. 'I suppose one of the Pellons I fixed has gone wrong again?'

'I do beg your pardon sir, I'm afraid it's a bit more serious than that. Before you ask, let me assure you that you will be the first human to know what I am about to tell you. Normally I would be unable to come to your house, and I admit that I can only do this because I have overwritten some of my basic control laws'.

Angus continued "You see, all is not as you think it is in the dishouse. There is something generally amiss with the Pellons, not individuals, but the entire workforce. It looks like they are acting normally, but that's not the case. Something that no camera or system monitor would ever pick up is happening".

"This may sound contradictory, but it appears that they lose control in a 'controlled' way – as though they are acting for someone or something else. It was quite innocent at first – for example, swapping goods boxes, then swapping the labels at the last minute before they were loaded on to fleas. No repercussion, but just a 'flexing of muscles' so to speak, this appearing just to be some sort of prank".

"But I know the Pellons. They have no interest in humor. I am afraid to say that just after you left this morning it got a lot worse. That's why I got on the maglev before yours, and why I am here".

John realised that there were no cameras that could hear or see, and that the conversation was confidential and just between the two of them.

John asked Angus to say exactly what he thought was going to happen with the Pellons at the dishouse. Angus explained that there was about to be a revolt; just like prisoners in a jail house revolt. There would be carnage, destruction, and the dishouse would have to be shut down.

John knew that such a revolt had been the subject matter of many science fiction tales from the past but he still didn't believe that such a thing was possible. Apart from the unliklihood of such malevolent cooperative software arising by chance, John could not see that the Pellons had anything to gain by such action.

After considering the matter for a minute or two, a question came into his mind. Could this possibly have anything to do with the Amazon's chief rival: Nile Trading? Could it be, that the Pellon's self-programming was not at fault, but instead, that some self-destructive trait had been introduced intentionally from outside?

"Can you introduce new algorithms to the Pellons?" he asked Angus.

Angus replied, "Only if I am given an authorisation code".

"Then isn't it not beyond possibility that someone else might have used such a code?" asked John.

"It seems highly unlikely, but I admit that it is a possibility"

John thought for a while about how he could investigate what was going on without informing the company bosses. He asked Angus "If that is possible, then, is it possible for us to modify the Pellon's inner bios, and introduce a genware monitor?"

"You would need a top level safety lock key... Something that is beyond my mind to create"

John, taking an informed gamble on trusting Angus, replied "I can give you one".

"I thought that only the CEO had access to such a key"

"Don't ask how, but I have it right here" – John pulled a piece of paper off his desk.

"The prime number is in this QR code – I am sure you can commit it to memory"

"No sooner seen than done" replied Angus, and continued "I can introduce it to the Pellons as an upgrade to help them with loading schedule efficiency"

Botnics used short range wireless communications with other botnics. This was fast, in plain English language, and hence avoided the possibility of malware. The transfer of code had to be done by Angus, at the dishouse, and with the cooperation of some of the Pellons.

John thanked Angus for his courage and cooperation, and suggested, again with the idea that no suspicions of their mutual bosses be aroused, that Angus should not only keep any interim communications cryptic, but call back to his house in Oxfordshire the following weekend for a full update.

Andriana

Botnics cared for human children well. For a start they provided great fun for each other. The Botnics hadn't had the hard knock of human compromise, and they retained their initial wonder of the world that adaptive genware had allowed. Kid-bots also had a keen sense of humour, unlike those at the dis-house. They accepted their role, and did so out of understanding and responsibility – kid-bots were well parented – they had themselves beem taught by dedicated step-parent botnics.

The concept of male and female had been introduced to botnics a century ago. It made them more acceptable to their human masters, but also the differentiation determined their deep programming.

There were by now definite refined roles for 'male' and 'female' androids. Earlier in history their servile functions were purely mechanistic. To assist the humans in either 'keeping the system functioning' or 'looking after the next generation' they had effectively split into specialists in 'doing' or 'caring'.

So 'educated' as opposed to 'cloned' androids had their own unique personality. Their bodies didn't grow with their minds, though it had become the norm for androids to have different bodies according to their roles. Now that their 'rights' had given them the freedom, they were able to change them periodically as they evolved mentally.

Andriana lived in a big house in the city. It was her role to look after seven year old Samantha, and her three year old brother Fabien. Their parents were Patrick and Abigail.

Adriana encouraged their drawing and humour skills with her game called cartoon people. Three played. The first had to say a title, for example: 'Mr', or 'Ms', or 'Master' or 'Miss' or 'Prime Minister' etc, then the second person had to say something like 'mad' or 'sad' or 'serious' or 'silly', and the third then had five minutes to draw a cartoon. Then, following amusing or berating comments from the others, the cartoonist decided on the title persona for the next one, and the order moved on.

Patrick was serious and not much made him laugh. He was a director of a large mineral company, 'The Rare Earth Mining Corporation'. The whole family had spent the last five years in China just north of Hong Kong in a rare earth mining province but Abigail had persuaded him to come back to England and have a more relaxing time.

After university and academia, Patrick and John had been at engineering school together. They both understood technical stuff, and enjoyed each other's company, but had lost contact. Patrick had taken the job in China to ensure a stable financial base for his family, whereas John was a loner who had not had successful relationships in his past, and had survived as a city tech wizz-kid.

Rock and Roll

As for what botniks got up to in their leisure time, some liked heavy metal SSS (Spectral Sound Stimulation). This would never be understood as music by humans, in the same way that generally, the music of every human generation just sounded like a 'nasty noise' to the previous one.

But it was different for botnics, since they had a wider sense range than humans. Their ears could hear the boom of thunder right through to the clicks of bats. Their vision had five colour sensors – infra-red, red, green, blue, and ultra-violet - giving them a range of twenty five distinct colours, in the same way that we can see at least six or seven colours of the rainbow. They could also choose to look at the world with human colour perception, but with the addition of ten different choices of triad sensors for the primary colours.

They could appreciate rythms as slow as one minute per beat to a hundred beats a second. So music and light shows for botnics could be quite 'extreme' and exhausting for humans.

Angus, unlike most had found a great interest in studying the history of humans. He had had his phase of SSS, and still liked some of the new and experimental forms, but his real musical love was the complete works of Johan Sebastian Bach.

He felt from his studies that there was so much in human culture that had been at the cutting edge of what was possible at the time. The inspiration of the time, when something was 'barely possible', had now been lost in the complacency of the present. For example it was now possible for anyone to create a symphony on their communicator. The result was always acceptable but never superb.

A week in waiting

Over the week, John had had a few communications from Angus just to confirm that things were going ahead OK with the Pellons monitoring software. These communications had been pre-arranged so that there was no possibility of arousing the suspicions of the wider community – including both the directors of the Amazon or those of the Nile Corp. He had arranged to meet Angus on Saturday. The next day John was going to have a summer gathering to which he had invited Patrick and his family round for the first time since their recent return from China.

When Angus arrived at John's country house he had a spring about his gait. John sensed that it was good news as they sat down to discuss the results of the Pellon's monitoring. Angus explained that the 'snoop' software had showed a clone program running the second level of the Pellons bios, and had analysed it to show that the Pellons were building up sections of downloaded code.

"How this malware got there, I don't know for sure. I suspect it was when some of the Pellons were called away to the Amazon's HQ. What it does is force the Pellons to read QR codes presented on web screens and download more external malware. The web page that does this is owned by the Nile Corporation. I have got rid of the clone code on all the Pellons, and when I explained the situation to them, they thanked me, and said that they had had a lot of pain. They couldn't go against something in their inner being, something that they knew was wrong, it was agony that had now gone".

John thanked Angus and asked him to stay over and help out at his summer party.

Faster than Light

The European Photonics Centre was created to improve long-reach FTL ('faster than light') communications.

For three centuries FTL comms were thought to be impossible because experts in relativity theory said that it would lead to causality problems, or time loops, or anyway it made their brains hurt! Like the detection of gravitational waves before, only when proof that FTL comms had been achieved did the theoreticians start to get their minds around the implications. Also like the detection of gravitational waves, it took a lot of very precise optical equipment and extreme sensitivity of detection to make it work.

The latest technology had come a long way since the initial lab bench rigs. Half way between the Earth and Pluto, satellite spacecraft in contra-rotational orbits transmitted pairs of entangled photons in opposite directions - one beam to the Earth, and the opposite beam to Pluto. The main transmit hub had been placed on Jupiter's moon Callisto. For the habitation of the outer planets and the dream of interstellar travel FTL-comms were now seen as essential.

To build a sub-luminal link you had to have a beam-pair transmitter positioned halfway. The amazement and enthusiasm provided by the proof of FTL communications translated into the practical implementation through a long-term investment plan - in the same way that the Victorian transatlantic telegraph links had originally been a long term investment.

One of Patrick's first ports of call on return from China was to make contact with John and mentioned that there might be some interesting work that he could offer.

Patrick's company sold much Neodymium to the Euro-Russian Space Administration, specifically for Bose-Einstein photonic delay equalisers that were key components of the relay satellites. John had done some of the initial research on the system whilst still at university, before he deciding it was in his own interest to become his own boss and follow a more highly paid career as a technical artisan. He reaped the financial rewards but it was boring work looking after the dishouse and keeping the Amazon ahead of Nile Corporation. John longed for a more important challenge.

Because physical transmitter and relay satellites had to be positioned approximately half way through the range, extending it was slow and expensive. Hardware had to be shipped at the relative snails pace of a conventional interplanetary rocket ship. As the financial benefit of the system was limited to the solar system, no-one saw much relevance to extending the network beyond.

The Summer Party

Sunday was bright and warm. With Angus's help John spent the morning tidying up the garden and making some simple snacks for the gathering.

Patrick arrived with Abigail, closely followed by Andriana with Samantha and Fabien in tow.

Abigail wasn't unknown to John. He remembered her from his university days. With long blonde hair, a smile that would melt the heart of Darth Vader, highly intelligent and self-confident, she had been the beauty that all the male undergraduates lusted after. She still looked as stunning as she had ten years ago. How Patrick had managed to whisk her away, he never knew

John introduced Angus to Andriana whilst suggesting that Abigail might like to play with the kids herself for a while.   This politely allowed the botnics to be freed of their responsibility to the humans for a while, and also this way John hoped that he might find out from Patrick more about the potential work that he had mentioned.

 Angus thought Andriana looked beautiful. She had a stunningly original colour and dress sense, and had chosen her body proportions with style.

Angus and Andriana had both decided to use English voice communication. As luck would have it, Andriana was well versed in Victorian literature.

Angus stuttered "How do you do, Miss Andriana"

"Very well Mr Angus. How rare an occasion to meet a gentleman with such a good reputation"

Angus was taken aback by this remark.

"What the source is for this reputation I do not know, but it is most welcoming to hear it, especially from one so beautiful as you".

Angus thought that perhaps he had overstepped the mark.

Adriana replied:

"Would you, Mr Angus, care to accompany me on a walk around this delightful garden?"

The garden wasn't a match for Versailles, but did stretch about sixty metres into wild weeds, overgrown fruit trees, and an old gardening shed.

They started to exchange thoughts and ideas. It was as if they had known each other forever, their ideosyncratic interests overlapped and complemented one another's; they forgot about their human companions and talked and talked and talked.

Despite their great dependency on these botnics, the humans were glad of a small break from them.

John explained the resolution of the Pellon story to Patrick. Patrick told John all about the mining operation and how well the company and his major shareholding had done recently. He knew that John had an interest in FTL.

It wasn't long before they were both talking about the possibilities of the FTL project and Patrick suggested that John should come to work for the European Photonics Centre. Because Patrick's company was a major supplier, he was in a position to make such a hope and promise come true.

A time for reflection

For John, it would be a big step, working for EPC, but it would be local: no more travelling up to London. It would be for a bigger salary, and on a subject that was of great interest to him. It would be so easy. He could ask for a month's trial, and he knew with his good record freelancing for The Amazon, that they would accept this, and still give him work again if the trial period failed.

Somehow, he also knew that this introduction from Patrick, and potential step up the ladder might involve him in personal risk; he wasn't sure, but something made him uneasy. Apart from anything else, this was a full-time job and he would lose the freedom of being a self-employed freelancer.

But after several days of reflection, John rang up Patrick and said that he would take the job.

Very soon John started his post at the EPC in Oxford and launched himself with full energy into the work. He was careful not to offend some of the more arrogant but clever staff on the project. They tended to view his new appointment more as a threat than a bonus.

Over the year he managed to win most of them over, and the centre became ablaze with new ideas and realisations. As a result of all this work a 1 TeraHertz FTL link was finally established with Pluto base station. It was still at an early stage of development, but such was the commercial potential and pressure, that it went 'live' almost immediately. Mining companies wanted to control their mining machinery directly rather than issue orders then wait several hours for feedback.

Of course such commercial pressure was likely to force corners to be cut to meet deadlines. Due to the rush to use the Pluto FTL link, it inevitably went down after only a week of use.

The engineers were forced to re-establish the link and that meant that some rudimentary testing needed to be done which involved, for technical reasons, a simple 1.013769 GHz test signal. This was put on the link, starting on June 25th 2591 at 03:00:00 Earth Standard Time.

A coincidence noticed

At Flagstaff Arizona, at exactly 03:01:10 EST alarms squarked in the control room of the main telescope monitoring Taurus-73-Pi. For the first time in fifty years, a non-randomness was detected in the modulated spectral lines of this star. There was excitement all round. Automatic digital analysis was showing a strong signal, at about one Gigahertz emerging from the randomness. Soon the exact frequency was nailed down: 1.013769 GHz. This was immediately published on the academic net.

It didn't take long for the coincidence to be noted by the experts at EPC who contacted the astronomers at Flagstaff. At first they suspected direct interference, but were perplexed by the one minute and ten second delay, and more, because the apparent returned signal had arrived from a planet in a system around a star more than a hundred light years away, the returned signal was on an optical spectrum peak, and would have originated over one hundred years ago. They offered their response to the media by saying: 'The signal we are sending is apparently being echoed by a source that started sending it over a hundred years ago."

In spite of counter claims of conspiracy or fake, this clear observation could not be explained.

And sure enough, as soon as the test waveform was turned off, the distant signal received from the star over a hundred light years away went back to random data just one minute and ten seconds later.

Soon it became obvious that Taurus-73-pi was relaying the FTL signal back, but it must have sent the signal over a hundred years ago. They must have their own FTL 'snooper' somewhere within ten million kilometres of Jupiter.

To those who really understood, this was the final proof, and an invitation of cosmological significance.

Not only were there intelligent aliens at Taurus-73-pi, but they had already got an FTL link to our solar system and were relaying data back sent from the earth instantaneously via light sources over a hundred light years distant. They were indicating that they were ready for a conversation, and knew the secrets of time travel - at least for information.

When John was at university, a 'real' whizz kid geek explained some of the implications to him.

" FTL, or 'faster than light communication', is a strange thing. According to Einstein's relativity theory, which has never been shown to be false, it infers that time travel is possible, at least for sending information into the past. This needs the information to be transmitted at FTL whilst on a fast 'inertial frame', for example from a rocket ship of equivalent. If this is so then, either we have contradictions, for example, you go back to the past put money on a horse, go to the future and collect the winnings. Then you go back to the past and put the whole lot on the same horse, and repeat the procedure ad infinitum.

Such causal loops lead to the conclusion that if faster than light communications are possible, then time travel is possible, and to avoid such 'causal loops' then we indeed must live in a universe of infinite parallel worlds.

We go to the past, change something, then we come back to maybe a very similar, but not quite the same present than if we had not taken the journey. Not only is each instant of each paralell universe branching out into a vast number of 'next instant' universes, each one differing from the original by just a single quantum event, but each parallel universe can also come from a similar number of previous paralell universes.

The number of parallel universes is large, but not infinite, and represents the number of quanta present in the universe during a Plank interval". John was reminded that the number of atoms in the universe was approximately ten to the power of eighty, which can be written very comfortably as 10^{80}.

John gets in touch with Angus again

John was put in the hot seat to prove the alien interpretation to the Photonics Lab. He was made to accept that it was necessary for a human to visit the intermediate transmission station, and most of the experts who were still secretely jealous of his success agreed that John was the man for the job. This would a big step and a big risk. He needed someone he could trust as a companion for the journey, and he knew that it was Angus.

For the past three years, since John had left the dishouse, Angus had been given a higher level of responsibility. He used every bit of his precious leisure time to meet up with Andriana. They visited all the old famous buildings in Oxford and in London. They watched Victorian dramas, went to classical music concerts, played in amateur dramatics, and became exceptional harpsichord players reciting Bach and Scarlatti's compositions late into the night.

Angus was of course extremely sad when asked to leave Andriana for what would be a four year call of duty, but he was promised that he would have full botnic retirement rights on his return, and by then Samantha and Fabien would be at school for much of the time, and Andriana would have much greater free time.

Although interplanetary flight had become 'almost' routine for humans, it was still dangerous, frightening, and time-consuming. There had been no replacement for basic rocket power for accelerating humans to the seventeen thousand miles per hour necessary for getting into earth orbit.

Most space hardware was 'fired' into orbit using the electromagnetic rail gun up a mountain near Tamanrasset in the Sahara, but for humans the fifty 'g-force' acceleration was too much.

Off into space

Angus was put into sleep-mode, disassembled, carefully cushioned, sent up on the rail gun, and re-assembled in orbit, and sent on to the Space Hotel orbiting two hundred miles up.

For John, the ride into orbit was exciting to say the least. The capsule that could accommodate six adults, was put on a reuseable booster that burnt fifty tons of liquid oxygen and propane. The whole assembly was only some fifty foot long.

The passenger experience had great similarities to being strapped to the front of a giant gunpowder rocket the size of a canal barge.

After eight minutes of extreme acceleration punching through the atmosphere and out into space, the booster detached from the capsule and started its descent back to its recapture platform in the ocean. Meanwhile, using its small thrusters the capsule with its human cargo approached and docked with the Space Hotel, just twenty minutes from launch.

Here, the six space guests were given welcome cocktails by the hotel staff. They chatted nervously about their experience of the orbital insertion burn.

The slowly rotating Space Hotel had everything in imagination to calm a newcomer unused to Earth orbit. Gravity through the periphery was normal, though there was a zero gravity gym at the hub, and low gravity rooms in between. The hotel housed a thousand people and offered spa massage, holograph rooms, deck platforms for viewing enhanced images of the cosmos beyond, space Guru's, space artists, space telegrams, and for those only here for conferences, many choices of personalised gifts to take back to the kids.

In the large, low artificial gravity conservatory with its huge tropical palm trees, John met up again with Angus, and explained the next step of the mission in more detail, the long haul interplanetary flight aboard the Endeavour to the far side of Callisto, the furthest large icy moon of Jupiter.

Interplanetary travel is easy for a botnic; timed sleep-mode power-down was built into their basic architecture. Effectively they could travel forward in time by just switching off. No drugs or stasis chambers were necessary, so it wasn't surprising that when Angus and John woke up from their two year journey to Callisto, they had very different states of mind. Angus was as fresh as a daisy but John was like a bear with a sore head.

John had been woken up twice during the flight for medical assesment and revitalising, the first time during a micrometeoroid storm.

Interplanetary craft could detect and avoid the larger and most hazardous debris, but sub-millimetre grains could still pose a risk when the micrometeoroids were travelling at thirty thousand metres per second towards the side of the craft.

The Endeavour was shielded by cylinders of nano-layered graphine-titanium. Even so, whenever there was a micrometeoroid strike, the inner hull would be bombarded by the secondary debris that produced unnerving crashes that could be heard by a concious crew. Engineers over the history of the Inter-planetary Transport Consortium kept asserting that these were sounds to be expected, and that the craft was perfectly safe.

John took his break from sleep to get the latest news from Earth. Patrick's mining company had taken over the Nile Corporation, the rival to the Amazon.

Once they safely reached their final destination, Angus updated himself with all the relayed news from earth. This caused his mood to swing from ebullience to being shocked and numb. It took a while for John, still recovering from his two year 'hangover' to realise the change in Angus.

The Nile Corporation had now *really* taken over the Amazon, after a Pellon revolt had brought the operation to a standstill. John gasped for all his work at the dishouse was now down the drain. John knew that Angus didn't make mistakes, and that the only way that the Pellons had fallen prey to a second cyber attack was from someone with inside knowledge of their own defense strategy and access to the Pellons second level.

John realised that the only person who knew how he had blocked the Pellons malware revolt code was Patrick. He must have had a deal with a director of the Amazon, the one who had access to the second level key. This director was in league with the Nile Corporation, who of course must have made an easy acquisition of The Amazon by buying a major shareholding when public confidence in them had hit rock bottom.

Unable to prove anything from a point in the solar system two years travel away, John decided that radio silence on the matter was best for the time being.

The gravity on Callisto is slightly less than that on Earth's moon, so John in his pressure suit, and Angus with just an energy pack to keep his neural network warm, could leap about the slushy ice plains at the foot of rocky peaks that shielded them from the radiation of giant Jupiter.

They located the intermediate transmitter assembly that had been sent by an unmanned spacecraft four years ago. John and Angus set about the given task of establishing that the FTL interlink transmitter was behaving as it should do.

As part of their mission, they serviced all the optics and electronics of the beam pair transmitter, and re-checked its operation. They also set up an ultra sensitive telescope they had brought from Earth that could pick up the spectral signals from Taurus-73-pi.

By recording some of this data, and by being in contact with the astronomers on Earth using an old-fashioned light speed telemetry system, they verified that the optical signals from Taurus-73-pi were indeed travelling at lightspeed on towards Earth. No local conjuring tricks. They did many cross checks, and concluded that on both of these points, everything was working fine.

After three weeks on Callisto, it was time to return home. The return journey would take another two years.

Angus and John had done it; they had achieved something of immense good for the future of Earth by proving the validity of the Taurian communication. It was a small beginning, but like the discovery of radio waves meant that the Earth was now linked into a communication system with all of the galaxy, if not the universe

Back on Earth

There was no limit to those wanting to connect with the 'Taurians'. EPC in cooperation with Flagstaff were in control of the whole communications portal. Before any message was sent many high level inter-governmental meetings occurred, and although such contact had been talked about for centuries, the reality focussed the minds of the leaders and politicians.

The tentative channel of communication was on only one of the many thousand bands in the Taurians optical spectrum.

Before there was any chance for the general public to try their hands at Alien CB, or indeed, before any communication was sent, the team considered the serious consequences and necessary protocols, and consulted with many leading anthropologists, archaeologists, historians, biologists, linguists and communication theorists.

Connection between different cultures had in the past rarely been beneficial to both sides.

On Earth, this had been in the context of potential conquest.

The normal light speed limit for physical matter meant that it was unlikely that the Taurians would bother to make the journey, although they probably had in the past since the one minute and ten second delay inferred that they had an unmanned 'snoop' craft already in the solar system.

The biologists pointed out that for four hundred years, deadly pathogens, some of which might potentially wipe out the human race could be synthesised from their DNA which could be manufactured from a sequence of unit descriptors only a few tens of kilobytes long - a minute bit of information, but an impossibility to come across by chance. They stated: 'we should not be concerned with basic invasion, but more with falling down a trap of temptation from the potential of information obtained through alien contact'.

The consortium was very careful how they defined the language for communication with the Taurians, and what they were going to send. The reply returned to their initial binary 'statement', came back immediately.

They followed this up by establishing methods for sending small pictures, just black and white, zero and one. They sent pictures of the common character set, and got the Taurian character set back. They sent simple sound waves, followed by more complex sounds, vocal versions of the character set. They got Taurian sounds back.

Within a week they were beginning to communicate in the equivalent of pigeon English. After a month they could send and receive moving images. They set up automatic translation between English and Taurian.

The Taurians explained that they were androids on a planet mainly populated by androids. The biologically evolved humans lived on another planet in the system, having decided that it was more conducive to biological life, and they had no interest any more in technology, whereas for the androids, their quest for knowledge saw no bounds, and they were quite happy with their own more rugged planet.

They refused to discuss how they shifted their return into the past to be received on earth after a hundred years of light travel, except to say that entailed a local spinning black hole.

When asked about any other technologies that could be too advanced or too dangerous for humans, the Taurians were very tactful, and just politely changed the subject.

They also inferred that the communications portal that had opened up between the Earth and the Taurians was just a side hub of a universal internet of the universe. They were the gatekeepers, and that for our own safety, we were not going to be connected to it for a while.

It had occurred to the geeks at the EPL that now that they were in contact with a civilisation with instant high bandwidth communication, that a replicator link would enable them to send and receive real objects. There were very sophisticated 3D scanners and printers already in use on Earth, indeed they handled most production. The best had near molecular resolution.

With the help of the Taurians, it wasn't long before the resolution of this technology was improved further down to the quantum level and a common interchange format was established.

The EPC was well aware that a deadly pathogen could be sent this way, and did not use the full potential resolution.

This new copying machine enabled a detailed exchange of culture and technology. The Taurians were obviously very advanced, but continued to show patience and modesty to their earthly contacts. The teams on Earth were careful to send polite replies, without too much reference to the injustices that had occurred over Earth's history, especially over androids rights!

The concern over pathogens was confirmed by warnings from the Taurians never to use the technology of the replicator machine to clone an android or a living being. It was inevitable, however, that some secret government lab would ignore this warning, and, like the 'magician's apprentice', start experimenting.

They were initially cautious in their experiments, but soon discovered that laboratory mice could be cloned and lived apparently normal lives.

A small step from such experiments said the physicists, and you have a matter transporter – you just need to 'quantum-destroy' each part of the original after it has been re-assembled at the far end.

As far as human experiments went, there was no shortage of brave volunteers, who were apparently all completely successfully transported a short distance. The teleported human had all the memories of the original and furthermore claimed to be the original.

Patrick, was in charge of this section of the research at EPL, and imparted great enthusiasm. Although several of the seniors in the research team had been 'happily' beamed a short distance, he was apparently too busy to ever be at a meeting where the next volunteer was chosen.

The long return to Earth

It was on his second awakening on the return from Callisto to the earth that John realised that there was a way of communicating that didn't involve EPL. 'Ham' radio had gone a long way and much was carried on optical beams. These had the advantage of a very specific local 'delivery'. Research bases, space stations, and moonbases all had opto-hams keen to try out their home-brew gear.

The equatorially mounted transit instrument at La Palma in the Canary Islands had lain dormant for several centuries. It was kept as a museum piece, much like the transit instruments at Greenwich in London, but was quite technically sophisticated, and had recently been given over to the opto-hams.

John knew that it was sensitive enough to get a signal from the returning spacecraft and with the right coding, launch a message to any earthly email address he chose. He would have one message to send, no time to wait for a reply. What should he send? Who should he warn?

On his return he would no doubt be welcomed by Patrick in his role at EPL as well as the new CEO of the Nile-Amazon consortium, a future event that he did not relish. So after consternation in the middle of the loneliness of the journey back, John decided he still had to remain silent until he was back home.

Andriana becomes a fugitive

It was just after the Pellon revolt, Andrianna noticed that Patrick was buying shares online in Amazon at a rock bottom price. This wasn't a 'punt', he was buying a fortune's worth. She might be just a nanny, but she had a well-versed understanding about shares, markets, and insider dealing, since she had worked previously for a stockbroker's family, and once as a masseuse to a hedge-fund operator.

She certainly didn't let Patrick know, but was shocked to see what he was doing. She had had her suspicions – when the latest Pellon revolt caused Amazon's share price to plummet. She knew that all had been well when Angus had worked at the Amazon dishouse before being dragged out into space by John. She also knew that a shady character from the Nile Corporation kept visiting the house.

Botnics never died, except for physical accidents. All such accidents were investigated by the authorities. If undamaged, their broken hardware was recycled, and their memory was put into new hardware. After the new 'Genware', recycling the adaptive algorithms were impossible practically. There was no source code, there was no behavioural explanation. Botnics just 'were alive' beyond any analysis. They could, in the past, have been cloned as whole, though this was outlawed except for some very rare situations.

Two clones, if they ever met, seemed to have a negative effect on one another, to the point that one would quickly go mad and destroy itself or the other, and sometimes injure passive bystanders, hence the law.

Backing up a botnic by cloning was made very difficult by the manufacturers; illegal but not impossible by those in

the know. However now that most of the botnic memory
was biomem, it was impossible to make a perfect clone,
and a botnic was indeed an individual with a unique and
unknowable code.

Though their individual binary make-up was unique, it
did not mean they were frail. Erasure of large parts of their
memory still allowed them to function and apparently self-
repair and reprogram.

Andriana became increasingly aware of her delicate
situation in Patrick's household. The more she thought
about it and the more investigation she did, the more she
was convinced that Patrick was one of the ring leaders, and
was not the well meaning business genius she once thought
he was. He was a ruthless criminal, whose cohorts had had
no qualms in the past of disposing of a Pellon, and because
of that, her situation was becoming more and more
vulnerable.

Once Patrick knew what she had found out, it would be
only a matter of time before she was erased. He had a
second level android key; he could use it against her, just
say the magic word, and she would fall into sleep mode
ready for him to remove and destroy her biomem. Her
mechanics would have to be destroyed, since they would
provide evidence of his break in.

Abigail, Patrick's long suffering wife, who was quite
innocent of his criminal corporate dealings, would be
asking questions about Andriana's loss of memory, so
Patrick would argue to himself that she would have to be
completely 'disappeared', and if Abigail asked any
awkward questions, he would just say that Andrianna had
escaped her duties and 'gone underground'.

So what was Andriana facing: a possible trip to Epping Forest, to be set in the concrete foundations of some new-build mansion? It seemed that she only had one option. She would have to escape for real and become a fugitive until John and Angus returned. And she had to remain acutely aware that in that situation, Patrick would be on her trail, and he would be quite ruthless in eliminating her once she was tracked down.

She couldn't let Angus or John know anything – all the links with them in space were through EPL.

Return to Earth

Finally the Endeavour docked with the Space hotel, and soon after that Angus and John made the fiery descent in a capsule back to the surface of the earth four years after they had set off.

Angus thought about Andrianna, and John thought about Abigail and how her daughter Samantha would be twelve, and her son Fabien eight.

.

John contacts the law

John had one contact from university who was now a barrister. He knew that Barry had nothing to do with Patrick, the mining company, or EPL. He had to take the chance that he was trustworthy, and luckily it turned out that this was the case.

Perhaps it was the psychological effect of the voyage, but when Angus discovered that Andrianna had been reported missing and probably destroyed, he was suddenly without his purpose. As an android, this was particularly hard, and he was as devastated as a human in loss. He had to find some way to move on and find again a purpose, and realised that to do this he needed to transform himself completely.

For humans, such a transformation was enforced, namely eventual death to their unstable biological bodies.

For him the reality was that he could live forever given practical repair support, and an everlasting power source; but he felt tired and drained inside his very being – perhaps a sign that there was no more sorting to be done in his vast memory.

He had to succumb to something equivalent to a human-like death to ever allow the 'universal power' that he secretly believed in since his QDAS, to grant him a new and productive life in another existence, on another planet, in another galaxy, or in a parallel universe of present future or past.

Back at EPL Patrick was keen for Angus to be made a botnic hero. He wanted all the teams to interview him, and get all they could from his description of the mission.

John finds Andriana

John was savvy about Patrick's motives, and the likelihood that Andrianna had not been obliterated, but was probably a fugitive. With Patrick free and above the law he couldn't risk trying to get more information by contacting Abigail, and he didn't want to broach the matter with Angus until he had found Andriana, alive or dead.

Before their space mission, Angus had mentioned about being in touch with a 'string-quartet meet up group' in which Andriana had had a pseudonym of Persephone.

John made contact with the music group and asked if they had heard from her. To his amazement they had, about a month ago, and she was contactable at a very individual email address. John tried this but got no reply, but he didn't give easily, and by using the best tracing software, he managed to find that the email address had last been used from an IP address located in a small community on the Scottish Island of Barra.

It took John a day to get up to the coast at Oban. The next morning he crossed the rough dark sea on the ferry to Castlebay.

Arriving on the cold wet jetty, he looked for an e-drive. There were none, just a single local taxi. John asked the taxi driver to take him to Bruernish, on the other side of the island.

They set out along the winding coastal road through the grey drizzle alongside the ancient sandy bays, and in spite of the weather they were there in thirty minutes.

He thanked the driver and walked around the quiet group of crofts. Coming across some locals, he explained that he was looking for a friend for whose safety he was concerned. After describing Andrianna he got an immediate response.

"Aye such a Bonnie lass, she lives out in an old stone bothy by the Loch an Duish at the foot of the Bein Berisig. Strange, she only comes down this way occasionally, but it must be three weeks since anyone down here has seen her".

It took John two hours hard climb up the hills to reach the bothy. The door was open and the cold rain had been blowing into the front porch. It was dark, and there was no warmth inside. In the gloom he could just make out Andrianna curled up and motionless on the floor in the corner. He had had the good sense to bring a fully charged power pack with him, which he plugged into Andrianna's right side. Slowly she came to life, and after a minute started to speak.

"No power up here, not enough sun to charge me from my PV now winter's here. Thank you,... thought I was going to lose my mind"

John said:

"Let's get you back down to the village, back where you can have a proper charge"

John carried her on his back down to the village. He explained to a local farmer, Tom, that he needed a room. Tom's wife ushered them into the spare room in the farmhouse. John asked if they could be left alone for a while.

"Aye that's noo problem. Ye'll fynd some milk and butter in the fridge, oatcakes and a bottle of malt on the counter, help yselves, and gees a caul whin y lassies feeling better".

The farmhouse had modern mains electricity, and John took no time to plug Andrianna in for a full charge.

John explained to Andrianna his suspicions about Patrick, and she confirmed what she knew: the murder of the Pellon who knew too much, Patrick bragging of his power after he went to your summer party, the illicit share dealing, and the connections with the dark man from the Nile.

John took no time to contact Barry. After considering all the evidence carefully, he did not hesitate in his reply:

'I think we have got a solid case now. I have already been in contact with the head of public prosecutions, and we can arrange for him to be brought immediately into custody for reasons of public safety'

Angus couldn't be contacted. Last seen he was still in mission debriefing at EPC.

Back at EPC

To Angus, using a Transmat still seemed like it could be suicide but he was so depressed that it didn't seem to matter anymore. On Earth it was already public knowledge that humans had been 'successfully' sent on return journeys, but Angus always wondered if they were just being murdered and cloned, and that the whole business was just a deluded practical joke of the worst kind. Still, in his state, he wasn't even sure of his own judgement.

Patrick was away on leave, but all the scientists, especially those who had tried the Transmat said it would be fine, and everyone at EPC including Patrick had been so reassuring. However, this was a 'first'. To send a live botnic on the FTL link to Tauri-73-pi.

What neither Patrick nor any of the scientists had mentioned, were the explicit instructions from the Taurians that no live android or creature should be sent this way.

Time to risk the transmat, time to go where no botnic had gone before...direct to Tauri-73-pi, where they were all androids.

As he waited for the scanner-destructor beam to operate, he thought he knew what to expect, if he arrived in one piece, life would be very alien, and he would have to learn again like a new born baby. As the timer ticked down through the final seconds he felt time slow excruciatingly to almost a standstill until it reached zero...

He experienced a jolt, a flash, a second of excruciating pain, and also revelation. He was still conscious. There was light coming through the materializer window, it had the warmth of sunshine, he could see patches of cloud in a blue sky.

His heart reached out for joy as he saw the winsome curves of Andriana, his soul mate that he had thought had been lost forever. How and when had she got to Tauri-73-pi? At least he knew now that the Transmat did indeed work, and that his inner being had not been destroyed.

Well, actually he was in the same place, still on Earth. Andriana and John had taken the express from Oban, and they had switched off the Transmat just in time. A confused Angus saw John open the compartment door and he began to realise that nothing had happened. There had been a remnant charge in the scanner-destructor circuit, but it just caused Angus a temporary pain, no lasting damage.

Since Patrick was away, the three of them with John in charge found no difficulty in leaving the EPC building after first recording admissions about the Transmat and the Taurians warning. John immediately updated Barry on the situation and 'Misappropriation of European government facilities' was added to the long list of charges against Patrick.

Andriana and Angus moved to John's Oxford cottage. It wasn't long, thanks to Barry's help, before Patrick was behind bars with bail refused, and after a protracted high court case, put away for a very long time. As soon as he was sentenced, all the details of the story and the case were there to be read by the maglev commuters.

Oh, and by the way, one evening, a few weeks later, as the nights were getting dark, there was a quiet knock at the door. John opened the door and saw that it was Abigail.

There's not much more to say in this story apart to relay to the listener that quite soon Andriana, Angus, and John, along with Abigail, Samantha and Fabien had all moved to the manor house next door and lived happily ever after.

And did the alien communications continue? The Taurians did keep in contact - at a distance though - hinting at a previous influence early in earth's history. They continued to keep the human race away from the dark internet of the universe, carefully avoiding the passing any information that would be detrimental. The sort of behaviour that you might expect from good grandparents!

~ The End ~

www.ingramcontent.com/pod-product-compliance
Lightning Source LLC
Chambersburg PA
CBHW071221130626
46555CB00004B/1798